D1337694

Why do hummingbirds seem to glow with neon fire? How do they manage to hover, power dive, and fly backwards or sideways? Where do these tiny bits of nonstop energy get their fuel?

In this book, you'll discover the answers to these questions and more besides, as we take a closeup look at many of the species that inhabit the New World. Through the words of hummingbird expert Bruce Berger, you'll learn why these birds have delighted and dazzled humans for centuries. Thirty-four unusual photos show hummingbirds from tailfeathers to gorget, and from the mountains of Alaska to the rainforests of Central America.

Humans have long had a passion for these fearless flying gems. Aztecs and Victorian ladies alike wore their tiny skins on cloaks and hats. These days, we've stopped wearing hummingbirds and started protecting them. Besides describing their life cycle, this book shows you where to see wild birds, which zoos offer aviaries, and how you can encourage hummingbirds to make your backyard theirs as well.

CLOSE-UP
A Focus on Nature

SILVER BURDETT PRESS

Published by Silver Burdett Press.
A Simon & Schuster Company
299 Jefferson Road, Parsippany, NJ 07054
Printed in the United States of America
10 9 8 7 6 5 4 3 2 1

Library of Congress
Cataloging-in-Publication Data
Berger, Bruce.
A dazzle of hummingbirds/by Bruce Berger
photographs by John Chellman . . . [et. al.].
p. cm. -- (Close up)
Originally published: San Luis Obispo,Calif.: Blake Pub., ©1989.
ISBN 0-382-24893-7 (LSB)
ISBN 0-382-24894-5 (SC)
1. Hummingbirds--Juvenile literature.
[1. Hummingbirds.] I. Chellman, John, ill.
II. Title. III. Series: Close up (Parsippany, N.J.)
QL696.A558B47 1994
598.8'99--dc20 94-30869
CIP
AC

A dazzle of Hummingbirds

TEXT
Bruce Berger

SERIES EDITOR
Vicki León

PHOTOGRAPHS
John Chellman, Kay Comstock, Michael Fogden, Clayton Fogle, Jeff Foott, John Gerlach, François Gohier, Marcia Griffen, Richard Hansen, Stephen Krasemann, Wayne Lankinen, George Lepp, Pat O'Hara, L.L.T. Rhodes, Doug Wechsler

DESIGN
Cathi Von & Ashala Nicols-Lawler

Hummers~ Nature's tiny superlatives

Among the most unlikely citizens to greet the first Europeans in the New World were hummingbirds. Here was a bird smaller than any known in Europe. Yet it could fly forwards, backwards, up, down, sideways, or sit in sheer space between its blurred wings, calm in the air as a fish in the sea. Flashing in flight, these creatures sizzled with gemstone fire: emerald, sapphire, topaz, and ruby. Bolting from flower to flower, perhaps looking the first explorers right in the eye before spiraling out of sight, they must have seemed like fragments of a waking dream. Pilgrims who wanted a longer look could inspect the specimens adorning the ears of the Indians who came to meet them. Conquistadores no doubt admired their colors at the Aztec court, where dignitaries wore cloaks made entirely of hummingbird skins.

Further acquaintance has only given us new superlatives. Their size, for instance. The 2¼-inch-long Cuban bee weighs in at two grams, ranking with the pygmy shrew as the world's smallest warm-blooded vertebrate. Even the largest hummingbird, the 8½-inch Patagonia gigas, weighs less than an ounce. They have the most rapid wingbeats of all birds, the largest ratio of heart to body size of any mammal, and a heartbeat – up to 1,260 beats per minute – second

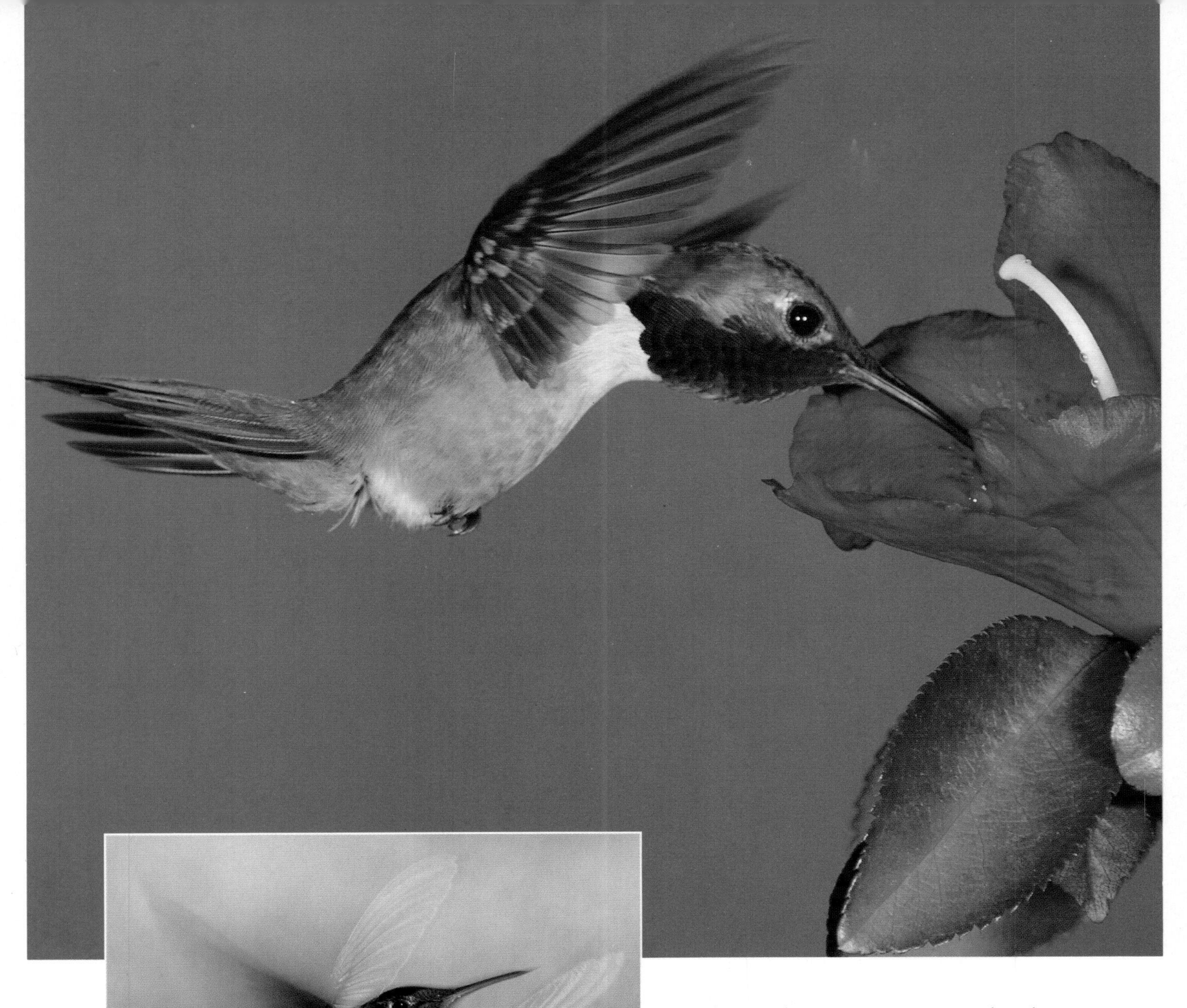

only to shrews. Hummingbirds possess both the most densely distributed plumage and the fewest feathers. Their tiny brains, 4.2 % of body weight, are proportionately the largest in the bird kingdom. But it is their energy output, the highest per unit of any warm-blooded animal, that impresses us most. Hovering they expend, relative to size, ten times the energy of a man running nine miles per hour. If that same man weighed 170 pounds and wanted to live the life of a hummingbird, he would have to burn 150,000 calories a day and drop 100 pounds per hour in perspiration.

Unknown in the Eastern Hemisphere, the

Trochilidae, as hummingbirds are known, ply the Americas from Alaska to the Straits of Magellan. With 343 species, hummingbirds make up the Western Hemisphere's second largest family of birds. More than half the hummingbird species are concentrated in the equatorial belt, ten degrees wide, across northern South America. Ecuador alone has 163 species. Hummingbirds are not as tropical as this distribution would suggest, being less abundant in the rainforest than in the Andes, where they range up to 15,000 feet. We clearly see this zest for heights in the United States, which has 15 species in the mountainous West and a single species east of the Mississippi River. Those that do adapt to rainforest tend to stay put, while species in temperate zones migrate. Most hummingbirds in the United States spend summers at the northern extremity of their range, repairing to Mexico, Central or South America as soon as the air gets nippy and the flowers few.

Tiny yet incredibly complex, the hummingbird appears to be operated by silicon chips. It can move instantaneously in any direction, start from its perch at full speed, and doesn't necessarily slow up to land. It can even fly short distances upside down, a trick rollover it employs when being attacked by another bird. Soaring with wings held still is the only avian trick not in its repertoire.

Rufous Hummingbird

Summer Range

Winter Range

Fall Migration

What do hummers and helicopters have in common?

Both can hover, take off and land vertically – even fly sideways and backwards. A hummingbird, however, rotates each of its wings in a circle, enabling it to fly in any direction. Choppers fly using rotating blades.

Hummers call many habitats home. East of the Mississippi River, ruby-throateds favor gardens and woods.

Its wing mechanism involves more firsts. Up to 30% of the bird's weight consists of flight muscles. The shoulder joint resembles a ball and socket, letting the wing rotate 180 degrees. The up stroke in most bird species simply returns the wing to its place. In the hummingbird, it adds propulsion and lift. To hover, hummingbirds move their wings forward and backward in a repeated figure eight, much like the arms of a swimmer treading water. Up stroke and down stroke match, pinning the bird in place. The tail helps steer, serving as rudder and brake.

As a rule, the smaller the bird, the faster the wing, and hummingbirds have the fastest wingbeats of any class of birds. That doesn't make them the fastest flyers. They move at roughly the same speed as songbirds and pigeons. Their small size, however, gives the illusion of greater speed. Their top velocity has been difficult to determine. Wind tunnel experiments have only gotten the ruby-throateds up to 27 miles per hour, yet they have been clocked alongside cars doing sixty. In normal flight, ruby-throateds beat their wings a modest 53 times per second, but in courtship dives they pour it on. Ruby-throated and rufous hummingbirds accelerate to 200 beats per second during their dives, and

How is a hummer designed? *Built for power and dazzle, hummingbirds are little more than flight muscles covered with feathers. With beaks like swords and tongues like extra-long straws, hummers drink quantities of nectar each day. The tails of these high-energy birds are used for flight and for display.*

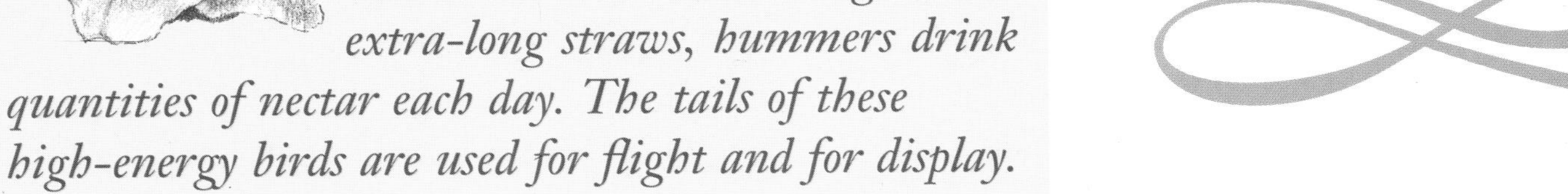

the Anna's and Allen's have been clocked in their dives going 60 miles per hour.

So dependent on aerobatics is the hummingbird that it can't achieve a proper walk. With its rather weak feet, it can manage minor hops, but uses its wings even to move down a twig or shift itself on the nest.

As specialized as the wings are the hummingbird's bill and tongue. It is believed that hummingbirds originally visited flowers for insects and wound up powering themselves on nectar. True or not, bird and flower have mutually adapted so well that bill and corolla fit like sword and sheath. In the United States, many flowers compete for a generalist like the ruby-throated, which has been seen feeding on 31 North American plant species. It is advantageous for such flowers to offer similar shapes. Hummingbirds that visit the United States respond with bills that are straight or slightly curved. The tropics, with many species in a small area, encourages specialization.

The bills of many hummingbirds curve downward, but two species have bills that curve upward. The aptly named swordbill has a bill as long as the rest of the bird. Astonishingly, a flower that was only conjectured because of a hummingbird's strangely curving bill was found to exist. The hummingbird's exploitation of the flower has led to its Spanish names, *chupaflor* and *picaflor* – flower-sucker and flower-nibbler – as well as the more romantic Portuguese *beija-flor* or flower-kisser.

Alpine meadows in bloom are home to several hummingbird species, including rufous and broad-tailed.

What do hummers eat?
In their non-stop quest for flight fuel, hummingbirds may visit 1,000 flowers a day. A long, W-shaped tongue helps them get to the bottom of each blossom. For protein, hummers eat spiders and strain gnats from mid-air.

The hummingbird feeds through a long tubelike tongue that darts deep into the flower's corolla for its nectar. The bird only seems to be drinking through a straw. The tongue is actually filled with a membraneous layer, and takes in liquid through capillary action the way a towel absorbs water. The tongue's brushy tip also traps insects on their own quest for nectar.

Plants that depend on the hummingbird for pollination do all they can to please. Their blossoms project into the open, where the bird won't get caught in foliage. Their trumpet shapes accommodate the long bills. Some flowers even provide grooves to ease the bills toward payload. Their long tubes, lacking perches at the lip, also discourage bees, butterflies, and other non-pollinating insects. Because hummingbirds have no ability to smell, flowers do not need to be scented.

Hummingbirds and human beings have similar color vision. Red – a color invisible to bees – flags their attention. Red predominates among the flowers the hummingbird visits, particularly in the United States, where flowers have hit upon common strategies. But hummingbirds will visit flowers of all stripes and colors. Their focus is nectar, not color. A flower's potency is measured by whether the hummingbird pauses for a nip or bellies up to the corolla. Ornithophilous or bird-loving plants – particularly in the tropics – wear the spectrum.

Hummingbirds feed on insects as well as nectar, both in the flower and in the air. Their thin bills are not well shaped for gathering insects in the

manner of swifts and swallows, but their pivoting flight compensates for that lack. They will also pull insects out of spiderwebs, including the spider itself. Sapsucker holes are a double treat, netting both insects and sap. Insects provide the hummingbird's protein. They can tide birds through winters when there are no flowers at all. Insects also furnish the fuel for baby hummers to grow. The ratio of nectar to insects varies from species to species, and is often difficult to determine.

Hummingbirds may seem to be Renaissance birds, good at everything, but in truth they make lousy singers. Most of them manage no more than a few mouselike chirps, squeaks and twitters, though they deliver them dramatically, with quick turns of the head. Hummers do make noise by zinging, a telephone-like sound produced by wings, not vocal chords. Each species has its own zing, rung by its own wingbeat. Biologists believe these sounds help hummingbirds communicate. The first species encountered by English settlers was the particularly loud ruby-throated, which gave rise to the term "hummingbird" and its German equivalent, *Schwirrvoegel*. Softer species have evoked such Caribbean names as *zum-zum* in Cuba and *murmures* in the Lesser Antilles.

Beyond size and maneuverability, the most astonishing quality of this bird is its ability to broadcast color. Hummingbirds seem to radiate like hot coals. Heads and throats flash magenta, then wink into black satin. Their throats or gorgets pass from copper to gold to green, performing alchemy before your very eyes. Like tiny prisms, hummingbirds twist and turn to reveal every color in the visible spectrum.

Anna's Hummingbird

All Year

Winter Range

Fall Migration

Most color that reaches our eyes is created by pigment, which absorbs some colors and rejects others. The colors of pigmented objects are, in fact, the colors those objects reject. The iridescence of hummingbirds operates by another principle known as interference. Pigment works by scattering light randomly from a single surface. Interference reflects light from two surfaces at once, synchronizing the waves from each surface. Light waves reinforce each other when they are in phase and weaken each other when they overlap. Out of phase, they cancel into darkness.

Tiny hairs called barbules create interference in hummingbirds. Inside each barbule are tiny plates, each made of two layers of a dark pigment called melanin with a layer of air in between: a kind of air sandwich. Some light rays bounce off the top layer. Other rays refract through the melanin (twice as dense as air), then reflect from the bottom layer in sync with the rays from the top layer. Light, passing through stacks of platelets that eliminate all other wave lengths, emerges as a beam of pure color.

Because interference projects in a single direction, like a beacon, the effect can only be seen at the proper angle. Not all the feathers with interference show color at the same time, but the surrounding black only intensifies the radiance. As soon as the bird turns its head, the beacon swings elsewhere, and the same feathers turn to soft coal. Different colors are produced by variations in the thickness and spacing of the melanin. So intricate is the phenomenon of iridescence, so like a set of Chinese boxes, that it can only be studied under an electron microscope. Structural colors are the purest, most intense colors we know. They cannot be reproduced by mechanical means.

Creating iridescence is such an effort that nature doesn't waste it. The most electric colors go onto head and throat. Only males show the deepest shades. Most hummingbird iridescence in the United States ranges from red to purple. Further south, it extends through many shades to the deepest blue. The metallic green backs of hummingbirds are also iridescent, but glow less brilliantly because the reflecting barbules are curved, scattering rather than reinforcing the light.

Why do hummingbird colors switch on and off? *Like soap bubbles, their color comes from iridescence, not pigment. It winks on and off, depending on the light source and the angle of the viewer. This allows hummers to flash colors or hide them – useful for males who want to impress females or threaten other males. Females have less biological need for color.*

Brilliant species like this red-tailed comet live in cool Central American cloud forest as well as tropical rainforest.

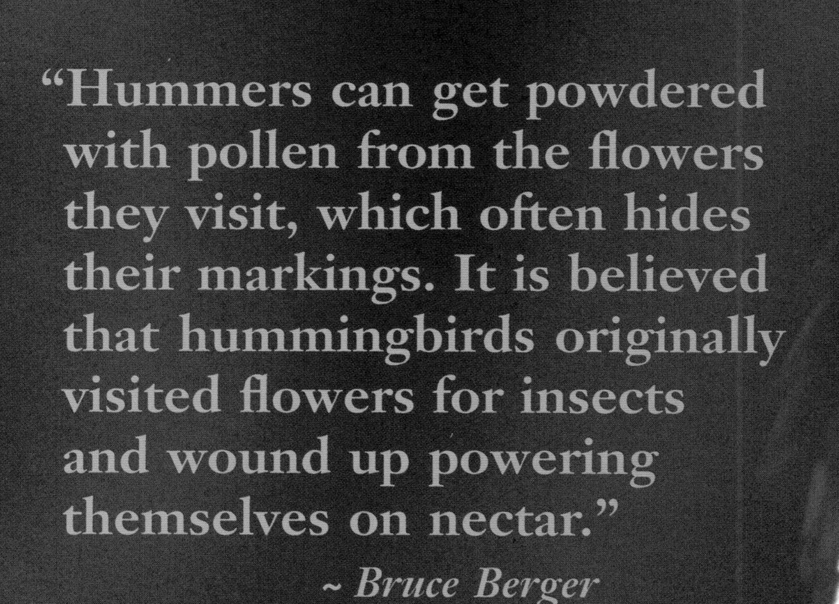

"Hummers can get powdered with pollen from the flowers they visit, which often hides their markings. It is believed that hummingbirds originally visited flowers for insects and wound up powering themselves on nectar."

~ *Bruce Berger*

Desert settings, from California's Anza-Borrego to the Rio Grande area of Texas, attract Costa's hummingbirds and rarer species.

Do hummingbirds mate for life? *No. In fact, most are single-parent families. During courtship, a male may impress a female by displaying colors, singing, or doing hundreds of dives. After mating, the female is on her own to make the nest and rear one – possibly two – sets of hungry babies.*

Hummingbirds also possess ordinary pigmentation in the brown tones. Some birds, particularly in thick rainforest where sunlight does not fall, can be drab as sparrows. But drab is the exception. Savoring their colors up close or through binoculars, you get the impression that instead of being named for jewels, it is jewels that should have been named for hummingbirds.

Anyone who has watched their diminutive skirmishes around feeders is aware that hummingbirds are aggressive loners. All of them have feeding territories which they defend from bees, other flower-loving insects, and other hummingbirds, regardless of species or gender. Migratory species that defend larger patches of terrain are more aggressive than those packed into tropical forests.

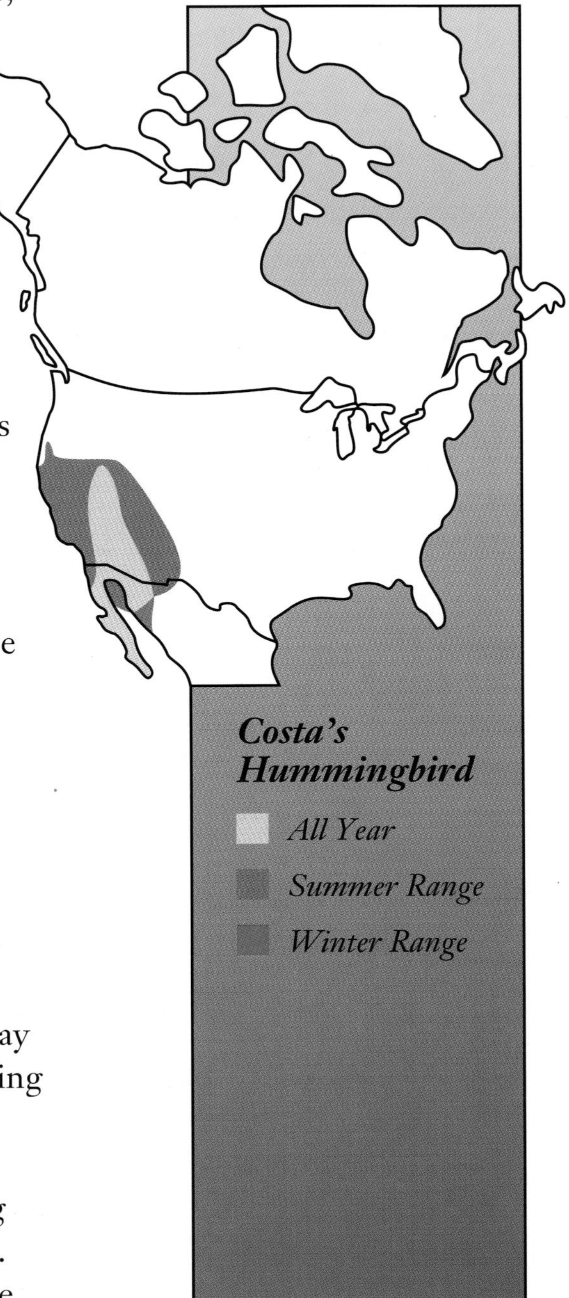

Usually content to threaten each other without physical contact, hummingbirds occasionally tussle in flight and fall to the ground. Hummers only abide each other when there is more than enough food. By concentrating their territories at a backyard feeder, you bring out their worst – and most entertaining – qualities.

Most hummingbirds come together only long enough to mate. A few species pair for life, but a whirlwind courtship usually substitutes for a lasting bond. Among migratory species common to the United States, the male performs an aerobatic display while the female hovers or sits watching, head flashing intently from side to side. The male ruby-throated, for instance, plunges repeatedly back and forth in a U-shaped trajectory, regular as a pendulum, making a smacking noise at the bottom to pop the question. Still more riveting is the dive of the male Anna's. He plummets toward the female at 60 miles per hour from up to 100 feet overhead, stops in front of her with a

How small is hummingbird small? *Some species are tiny enough to be mistaken for moths that also sip flower nectar. These eggs were laid by an Anna's hummingbird. Eggs from the Cuban bee, the world's smallest hummer, are even more minute. Ingenious hummingbird mothers use spider silk to anchor nests in place.*

booming of his tail, hovers facing the sun to show full iridescence, madly squeaking all the while, then shoots straight up to repeat the maneuver.

In the tropics where diving space is scarce, hummingbirds have developed a wholly different system. Though the hummingbird's least impressive quality is its voice, the males, unbelievably, court by singing. And because their voices are so feeble that the females would never find them otherwise, they sing in groups. Each courtship assembly or lek has from two to 100 males. Each male has his own perch, in locations that seldom change over the years. In a rare display of mutual tolerance, males line up and repeat what may only be a two-note squeak, over and over, while the females size them up. One species of hermit hummingbird actually sings its riff 12,000 times a day, every two seconds. Each visiting female eventually makes her choice, then the pair rockets away.

Some species court only by singing, some only by flight displays, some by assorted combinations. Such rites may seem capricious, but they serve a purpose. Courtship displays and promiscuity create a system that allows a dominant male to mate many times and pass on his traits. Evolution accelerates, leading to the diversity and specialization that create, in turn, more niches for hummingbirds.

Because of the speed and difficulty of following what happens after courtship, especially in rainforest, it is not easy to determine whether copulation occurs at the female's perch, at some other perch, or in flight.

In a few species that pair bond, the male actually helps with the rearing of the young. By and large, however,

hummingbird males are less involved with childcare than in any other family of birds. Immediately after mating, the female makes the nest. No location seems too humble for these knotty cups: twigs, vines, hanging leaves, the ceilings of caves. Spacing the nest well away from other females yet close to food sources are the critical factors. Nests can be finished in a day or fussed over for two weeks. Construction materials include plant fibers, seed husks, bud scales, shredded bark, insect galls, fibrous rootlets, cattail fluff, small feathers, wool, and the fuzz of the day. Thistledown, milkweed seeds, and the stems of young ferns soften the lining. Females stitch nest walls together with spiderweb silk, glue them with saliva, and disguise them with lichen and moss camouflage. If the perch is precarious, the nest is braced by mud on one side. I once watched a Costa's hummingbird build a nest on a ficus twig three inches from a windowpane in Phoenix. The bird hovered over the nest and stabbed new material in with her bill. Lighting on the cup, she craned backward and tamped each addition into place. Rotating around the nest with a whirring of wings, she shaped the exterior with the underside of her bill like an experienced potter, then settled on it like the lid of a doll's casserole.

A clutch of two white eggs is laid one or two days apart. No bigger than lime seeds, they are, unsurprisingly, the smallest in the bird kingdom. The mother incubates for 15 to 19 days, keeping the eggs covered 60 to 80% of the time. She leaves the nest only to feed and to fetch repair material such as cobwebs.

How do hummers keep clean? *Some shower in the rain or under waterfalls. Others use puddles or wet leaves to bathe. Hummers have tidy habits even when young. While still in the nest, baby birds begin to expel their wastes "over the side." Since their diet is mostly insects, they produce a lot of waste matter – most of it undigested insect parts.*

Born blind and with naked black skin, the young resemble raisins. They never do grow any down, but immediately sprout pin feathers. As they wait for mama to bring insects, their bills protrude from the nest like a pair of hatpins. At first she feeds them every couple of minutes. Later she slacks off to three times an hour, plunging her bill so swiftly and deeply into theirs that she seems to be goring their throats. After twelve days the young grow enough feathers so that she can stop brooding them for warmth. By the sixteenth day, they prepare for flight, flexing their wings and rising slightly from the nest. By the time they are completely ready to fly, they seem far too large for their space, looking like two castaways about to sink a life raft.

Twenty-five to thirty days seems a long stay in the nest, but it is common for birds that must be able to fly on the first try. They leave with no prompting, sometimes managing 50 feet on the inaugural flight. The mother still feeds them and checks up on them for a bit, but hummingbirds are short on family values and the young soon mature into loners. Mother has little time for sentiment either; often she is building a nest for a second brood while still feeding the first. It is a system that works, as I learned when I watched a Costa's hummingbird nest successfully in a loop of electrical wire leading to a bulb in a carport, indifferent to the comings and goings of cars, dogs, and human beings.

Hummingbirds have to be raised tough to maintain the dashing lives they lead. The species that migrate to the United States travel impressive distances. Many ruby-throateds, for instance, make a 2,000-mile journey each spring from Panama to Ontario, Canada. The trip includes a 500-mile nonstop flight over the Gulf of Mexico, during which the birds average 25 miles per hour for 20 hours. By adjusting the angle of their wings to benefit from prevailing winds, they clear the Gulf on a gram of stored fat.

By the time hummingbirds are ready to fly (at 25 or 30 days of age), they seem far too big for their space, looking like two castaways about to sink a life raft."

~ *Bruce Berger*

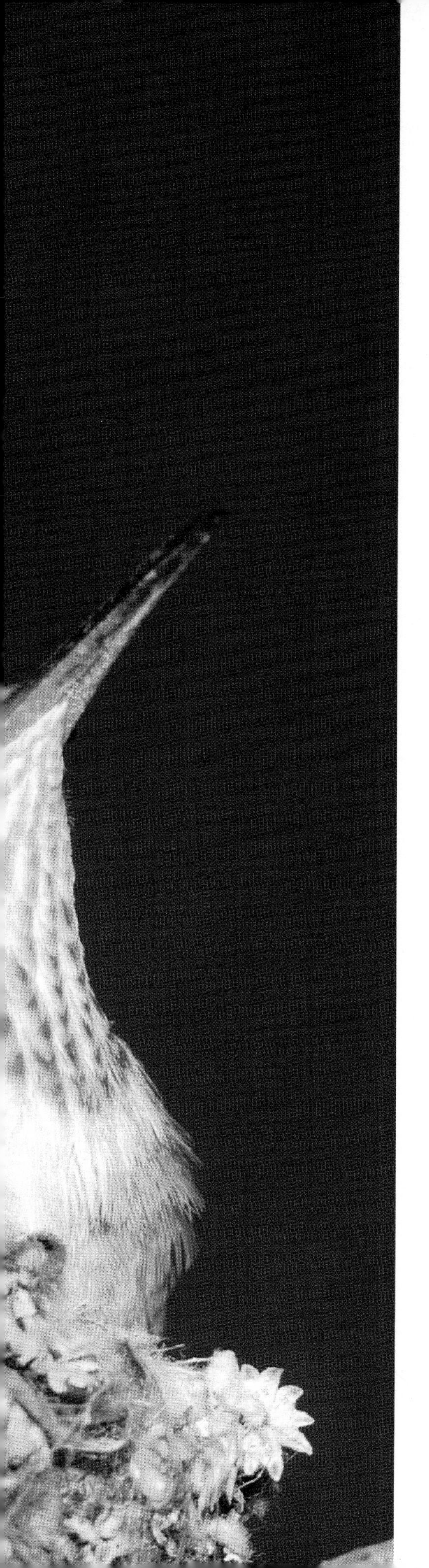

The rufous makes an even longer journey between the Mexican state of Guerrero and Alaska, where it ranges up to 11,000 feet. After breeding at the northern end of the circuit, this altitude-loving hummer returns south in a more leisurely fashion along the crest of the Rocky Mountains. The Anna's hummingbird remains in the United States by migrating vertically, breeding at low elevations during the California winter and spring, then heading to cool Sierra meadows for the summer.

Such demands take an extraordinary metabolism – 12 times greater than the pigeon, 25 times greater than domestic fowl. To maintain such energy, hummingbirds must feed every ten to fifteen minutes, 50 or 60 times a day. Their life is a relentless buffet, beginning before dawn and ending after sunset. Hummingbirds consume up to five times their weight in food and drink eight times their weight in water daily.

Being so small relative to their surface area, hummingbirds lose body heat rapidly. They also lack insulating down feathers which would cause them to overheat by day. To get through icy nights, hummingbirds sink into a torpor that brings their whole system nearly to a stop. For example, the Anna's hummingbird can drop its normal body temperature of 104 degrees to as low as 75. In torpor, the pulse of the blue-throated slows from 1,260 heartbeats per minute to a mere 36. During torpor, metabolic rate drops to one-fifteenth that of normal sleep. Because they need to keep their eggs warm, nesting females do not go into torpor. All other hummingbirds fluff their feathers and cool it each night until the chill is off.

Since miniaturization makes the fast life possible, you would think that hummingbirds would continue to evolve ever smaller. Hummingbirds and shrews, however, seem to have reached the lower limit for warm-blooded animals. Any tinier, and hummers

How do hummingbirds stay warm at night? *It takes lots of calories to fuel a hummer. To save energy, hummers have a special way of resting. At night (or any time they cannot get enough food to fuel themselves), they go into torpor – a state in which their metabolic rate is only one-fifteenth that of normal sleep.*

would lose heat too rapidly, become prey to large insects, and lose the structural strength of their bones. Hummingbirds are just small enough to have earned their French name: *oiseau-mouche* or fly-bird.

The French might just as well have called them little Napoleons, for they commonly chase crows, harass hawks, and pester bigger birds of all kinds. Since their bills are too fragile and important to risk in combat, hummingbirds dive-bomb their targets like insects. When they join forces with other small birds to plague raptors, hummers often lead the charge, feinting like tiny swordsmen.

In turn, these tiny bullies have few serious enemies. Smaller hawks sometimes kill and eat them. In a few recorded incidents, hummingbirds feeding at low flowers have been gulped by bullfrogs. There is also one astonishing eyewitness account of a hummer being downed by a leaping bass. Hummingbirds regularly eat spiders, occasionally becoming entangled in webs and ending up as the spiders' prey. In general, though, hummingbirds are vulnerable only in their preflight days. In the nest, they may be attacked by ants, rodents, raptors, and snakes.

As with other species, humans represent the most serious threat to hummingbird populations. Long before Europeans arrived, hummers had served as adornment for native peoples. But the heavy demand for hummingbird curiosities from the New World took a devastating toll, particularly in the Victorian era. Tough hummingbird skins made easy work for taxidermists. Hummingbirds were mounted on brooches, sewn onto hats, massed into dustcatchers, arrayed as artificial flowers, set on display under bell jars. In Brazil in 1888, over 3,000 topaz hummingbird skins were mashed together in a single barrel and shipped to London. One London firm sold 40,000 skins in a single year. A couple of hummingbird species, now presumed extinct, are only known from their service on Victorian ladies' hats.

With changes in fashion and laws that now restrict the trade in flora and fauna, the exploitation of individual hummingbirds has virtually disappeared.

Nor is any species currently threatened within the United States. The greatest problem the birds now face is human destruction of habitat, particularly rainforest. This jeopardizes the winter quarters for migratory species and evicts tropical species from their permanent homes. Despite field work, we still lack detailed information about many species' ranges and needs. Our best means of assuring a future for hummingbirds – and for human beings – is to leave such habitats intact.

Hummingbirds in the wild may live a decade, with the record in captivity being 14 years. Anyone with a feeder can tell you that either the original hummingbirds or their offspring return year after year with unerring accuracy, from whatever unimaginable distance, alert as ever. A few years ago I moved my feeder around a corner, thinking it might take them a day or so to relocate. They found it in seven minutes, then scouted the length of the eaves to see if the house grew feeders the way an apple tree grows apples. They take an uncommon interest in the orange knobs of my black deck chairs, and I have watched them explore my purple sleeping bag, in a vain search for the corolla.

At feeders hummers will sometimes light quite calmly on a finger that is substituted for a perch. They may lack outright affection for man, but their fearlessness and droll behavior make wonderful substitutes.

Just when you think they are out of surprises, you encounter them bathing. Much too independent to preen each other, hummingbirds still need to keep clean. They do so by hovering in waterfalls, in dripping foliage, in lawn sprinklers, in rain. They rub themselves on large wet surfaces, such as banana leaves. They sit in the water and splash like finches. In the mountains of Baja California I have seen Xantus hummingbirds gather below a one-inch waterfall until there were 11 of them lined up in a row. The sight of those tiny creatures all squeaking and splashing at once is as amusing a sight as I've seen in the natural world.

The world's best-known hummingbird must surely be the ruby-throated. Being the sole hummingbird resident in the eastern United States makes it easy to identify. It also has the most extensive literary coverage, beginning with William Wood, a New England colonist who wrote in 1634: "The humbird is one of the wonders of the Countrey... not bigger than a Hornet... as glorious as the Rainebow...."

My own favorite remains the tiny rust-colored rufous, which the sun turns into a cobweb of fire. He arrives at my feeder in the Rockies in late July, several weeks after the broad-tails have laid claim. Sitting like a bulldog on a nearby twig, he sips at leisure and lunges at all comers, even when he isn't interested in feeding. Devoid of charity, he is a most successful bird.

The easiest way to see hummingbirds is to bring them to your window with a feeder. Any model will serve, but those with a clear bottom show the snakelike darting of the hummer's tongue. If the birds are slow to catch on, attach a bit of red ribbon to attract them. Honey may seem a more natural sweetener, but it is too strong and will burn out their systems. Sugar and

"Anyone who has watched their skirmishes around feeders is aware that hummingbirds are aggressive loners. By concentrating their territories at a backyard feeder, you bring out their worst – and most entertaining – qualities."

~ *Bruce Berger*

Which hummingbirds are the rarest? *In the United States, the leading contender is the Xantus, a Mexican species that has been sighted (and photographed, above) in Arizona and California a handful of times. Lucifer is another rare species that occasionally dips north from Mexico.*

water in a one to four ratio approximates the nectar of the flowers.

If you want to draw hummingbirds to your garden, consider planting such flowers as tiger lilies, hollyhocks, phlox, fuchsias, gladiolus, morning glories, azaleas, nasturtiums, honeysuckle, columbines, and delphiniums.

A number of zoos and wildlife parks across the United States and in other countries have hummingbird exhibits, some of them walk-through, which allow you to see these little bits of almost-fluorescent energy at close hand. Other bioparks present habitats, such as desert or rainforest, where hummingbirds and other living things can be seen in more natural settings.

Whether you're in a park or your own back yard, ideal hummingbird viewing is in the wild. In southeast Arizona, a glorious concentration of species can be found in such beautiful corners as Ramsey Canyon, Cave Creek Canyon, Madera Canyon, Sonoita Creek, Guadalupe Canyon, and the little towns of Portal and Patagonia. Some, such as the rare Lucifer and violet-chinned hummingbirds, are Mexican species at the northern limit of their range. Others come to breed or feed in this plant-rich region where four habitats meet. At Mile-Hi/Ramsey Canyon Preserve, a magnificent slice of terrain has been preserved as a natural community forever by the Nature Conservancy, a national group dedicated to saving endangered species by protecting their habitats.

Among the desert cactus and sparkling wet canyons of southeast Arizona, humans can see and hear up to 16 species of hummingbirds. With luck and our continued stewardship, the zing of hummingbirds here and elsewhere will continue to dazzle and gladden future generations.

Ruby-throated Hummingbird

Summer Range

Winter Range

Spring and Fall Migration

John Chellman/Animals Animals: page 13
Kay Comstock: pages 30-31
Michael Fogden/Animals Animals: pages 20-21
Clayton Fogle: pages 14, 24, 26-27, 29, 34-35, 36
Jeff Foott: pages 8, 23
John Gerlach/DRK Photo: page 12
François Gohier: pages 2-3, 4 bottom, 9, 18, 28
Marcia Griffen/Animals Animals: page 40
Richard Hansen: pages 16, 27 bottom, 33 (both), inside back cover
Stephen Krasemann/DRK Photo: back cover
Wayne Lankinen/DRK Photo: pages 4 top, 6-7, 10, front cover
George Lepp/Comstock Inc: pages 1, 17
Pat O'Hara/DRK Photo: pages 10-11
L.L.T. Rhodes/Earth Scenes: pages 22-23
Doug Wechsler/Earth Scenes: pages 18-19

About the Author

Bruce Berger hangs his feeder in Aspen, Colorado. His essays have appeared in the *New York Times*, *Sierra* magazine, the *Yale Review*, and elsewhere, and have been collected in *The Telling Distance*, a Breitenbush Book publication.

Recommended Reading

Finding Birds Around the World (Houghton Mifflin), a terrific birders' guide with detailed maps to nature preserves and parks around the world; *Hummingbirds of North America* from Smithsonian Press; and *The Splendor of Iridescence* from Dodd & Mead Co. are also good.

Where to See Hummingbirds

The following zoos have a variety of hummingbirds on exhibit. Some, such as the San Diego Zoo and the Arizona-Sonora Desert Museum of Tucson, have walk-through habitat displays, with plants and a variety of species. Arizona-Sonora Desert Museum; Cincinnati Zoo; Denver Zoo; Los Angeles Zoo; Milwaukee Zoo; New York Bronx Zoo; Philadelphia Zoo; Phoenix Zoo; San Antonio Zoo; San Diego Zoo; Syracuse (Burnet Park) Zoo.

In the wild, visit such areas as Southeast Arizona, especially at Mile-Hi/Ramsey Canyon Preserve; Chiricahua National Monument; Saguaro National Monument (outside Tucson); University of Arizona campus in Tucson; in New Mexico at Gila Cliff Dwelling National Monument near Silver City.

Helping Organizations

Nature Conservancy, 1800 N. Kent Street, Arlington, Virginia 22209; (703) 841-5300.
National Audubon Society, 950 Third Ave, New York, NY 10022; (212) 832-3200.

Special Thanks

Norma Lee Browning and Russell Ogg; Kelly Cash and Debbie Collazo, the Nature Conservancy; David Butz, cover lettering.

Index

If you liked this book, we know you'll enjoy others in our nature series, including:

Hawks, Owls & Other Birds of Prey
Parrots, Macaws & Cockatoos
A Raft of Sea Otters ❖ *Seals & Sea Lions*
A Pod of Gray Whales ❖ *Sharks* ❖ *A Pod of Killer Whales*

The Habitat series:
Tidepools ❖ *Coral Reefs* ❖ *Kelp Forest* ❖ *Icebergs & Glaciers*

SILVER BURDETT PRESS

Published by Silver Burdett Press.
A Simon & Schuster Company
299 Jefferson Road,
Parsippany, NJ 07054
Printed in the United States of America
10 9 8 7 6 5 4 3 2 1